Rose's Big Decision

"You're arching your back, Rose."

Miss Coralie's voice made me jump. She was frowning at me, so I quickly corrected myself and she gave me one of her that'll-do nods. I sighed without letting it show. We were more than halfway through the lesson and I hadn't even got a nice let alone a lovely. That was gym's fault. But what am I supposed to do? Pleasing Miss Coralie and my gym teacher was impossible.

Ballerina Dreams

Collect all the books in the series:

Poppy's Secret Wish

Jasmine's Lucky Star

Coming soon:

Dancing Princess

Dancing with the Stars

Ballerina Dreams

Rose's Big Decision

Ann Bryant

USBORNE

My grateful thanks to Sue Downey
for all her help.

The publisher would like to thank Sara Matthews of
the Central School of Ballet for her assistance.

❋

First published in the UK in 2004 by Usborne Publishing Ltd,
Usborne House, 83-85 Saffron Hill, London EC1N 8RT, England.
www.usborne.com

Cover photograph by Ray Moller.
Illustrations by Tim Benton.
The name Usborne and the devices ♀ ⊕ are Trade Marks
of Usborne Publishing Ltd. All rights reserved.

A CPI catalogue record for this title is available
from the British Library.

ISBN 0 7460 6026 2

Printed in Great Britain.

1 Pulled in Two Directions

Hi! I'm Rose and I'm in a big hurry because I keep putting my leotard on the wrong way. First it was inside out and then back to front. This changing room should have a few more mirrors in it so people can see what they look like when they're getting changed. Then they wouldn't make mistakes. In fact, I think I might suggest that to Miss Coralie.

Actually, I know very well I *won't* suggest it to Miss Coralie, because no one in this ballet school would ever dream of suggesting *anything* to Miss Coralie. You don't talk to anyone during class and you *definitely* don't talk to Miss Coralie. When I think back to when I first started ballet two terms ago, I feel quite embarrassed, because I didn't realize about not talking and I just said anything I felt like saying. I didn't even want to *be* at ballet back then. I absolutely hated it. But then I met Poppy and Jasmine and gradually, bit by bit, I found that I quite liked it after all.

I'm not very good at it, but Poppy and Jasmine are giving me extra lessons to try to make me better. Then I'll be in the same class as them. Well, that's what *they* think. Personally, I think there's about as much chance of that happening as there is of the moon turning purple.

"You'd better hurry!" said one of the girls in my class, pushing open the changing-room door. "Miss Coralie's going to call us in any minute now."

I pulled my hair through a hairband and

scooped it round into a bun. "Can you save me a place in the line?"

She nodded and went out while I rammed a few hairgrips though the bun, then rummaged round in my bag for my shoes. I don't even know that girl's name because, when you only meet up once a week and you're not supposed to talk in class, you don't get to know people very well.

The reason I got to know Poppy is because we're in the same year at school. She was already friends with Jasmine but they kind of let me in, and now we're all best friends together. I call us a triplegang.

I pushed my hairband on and rushed out of the changing room, taking a quick glance at myself in the mirror by the door. What a mess! I hate my leotard. It's far too big for me and I look really silly in it. How come all my clothes are too big for me? Well, I know the answer to that. It's because I always have to wear my big brothers' old jeans and T-shirts when they grow out of them. I don't mind that too much, but I feel stupid wearing a leotard that's too big. I suppose it's my fault really. I shouldn't have refused to go with Mum to buy it. It's just that I was feeling so mad about having to do ballet in the first place that I told Mum there was no need for me to try on the leotard. She could just get one that looked as though it would fit.

"Come in, class," came Miss Coralie's strict voice as I squashed into the line in front of the girl who'd saved me a place.

We all started to move forwards in silence. When you get to the door you're supposed to run in on tiptoe to a place at the *barre*. I was all ready to do my best running when I happened to look down and notice that I hadn't tucked the little drawstrings into one of my shoes properly, so I quickly bent down to do it. Of course that made the girl behind fall into me, so I toppled forwards and didn't make a very good entrance.

Luckily, Miss Coralie was watching the girls at the end of the *barre* so she didn't notice me, but I think Mrs. Marsden, the pianist, did. I saw her frowning in my direction. I put my hand on the *barre*, then quickly took it off again because you're not supposed to do that until the preparation, so I concentrated on getting my hands in exactly the right shape, with my little fingers near my legs. Then I stood up straight in fifth position and said to myself what I always say to myself at the beginning of class. *Please let today be the day that Miss Coralie says* lovely *to me.* Twice I've had a *Good, Rose,* and three times I've had a *nice,* but they were all ages ago, and I've never had a *lovely. Lovely* is the very best word that Miss Coralie can say. It means she's really really impressed. I'd be in heaven if I got a *lovely,* but these days I just seem to get corrected.

"*Preparation* and..." said Miss Coralie. The music started and we all prepared to second then began the *plié* exercise as Miss Coralie watched us with her eagle eyes. She was walking slowly round the room, saying the counts to the beat of the music, and other things too, in the same rhythm: "And *one* and *two* and *lift* up *Becky* and *turn* out *Rose* and *seven* and *eight*..."

Pooh! I thought I *was* turning out. The trouble is that I'm doing so much extra gym at the moment that my feet aren't in the habit of turning out, because you work in straight lines for gym. I'll just have to concentrate harder than ever so I don't get mixed up and think I'm doing gym when I'm supposed to be doing ballet.

"...and *nice* work *Ellie*, and *close* in *fifth*..."

I was good at fifth position and I really focused on turning out and not arching my back, which is something else that Miss Coralie has started mentioning quite a lot recently. Surely I'll get a *lovely* now, I thought to myself, or at least a *good*.

Pulled in Two Directions

But Miss Coralie was completely silent, joining in at the front. I wished I could turn my head to watch her properly instead of out of the corner of my eye, because she looks like a real ballerina when she does dance steps. It's no wonder really. I mean, she was once a soloist with the Royal Ballet. I knew I mustn't turn and watch her though, because even your head has to be in a certain position for every single ballet exercise. There's so much to think about all the time.

"Soften your elbow, Rose. You're not doing gym now."

Oh, no! Not again! It seems like the moment I stop thinking about any part of my body, even for a microsecond, it goes straight into gym mode by mistake. It's really beginning to get on my nerves. Still, it'll be better once the gym competition's over and I go back to gym club once a week. Only two and a half weeks to go. A little shiver tickled the hairs on my arms when

I had that thought, because I'm quite nervous about the gym competition. But excited, too.

When we do centre work I have to concentrate even harder than for the *barre*. I've just about learned all the French names for the steps and the different positions and directions and everything, but, as Miss Coralie often says, it's no good just coming to class once a week, you have to practise at home in-between as well.

I'm lucky because Poppy helps me at school during break times and after lunch, and we often get together with Jasmine at the weekend too. All we ever do when we're together is practise ballet and talk about it, or dress up and make up dances and tell each other our ballerina dreams. Well, the other two tell each other their ballerina dreams. Personally, I haven't got any. That's because I'd never be good enough to be a ballerina in a million years, so I just listen to *their* dreams. And anyway, everyone thinks I'm going to be a gymnast when I grow up, which would be great. All the same, my mum and dad can't believe how much ballet has "grown on me" as Mum puts it, in such a short time.

It all started when I opened my birthday card from Granny and saw the little message inside, which said that her present to me was one term of ballet lessons.

I remember my jaw hanging so far down I wasn't sure that I'd ever be able to shut my mouth again. I really think I must have been the crossest, most disappointed person in the whole of England at that moment. But Mum was raising her eyebrows for me to say thank you to Granny, and Granny was smiling away so I had to swallow my crossness and try to look happy.

"Thanks, Granny."

"You don't have to pretend, pet. I know you're not impressed!" She'd chuckled like mad.

I'd really wanted to say: *No, I am NOT impressed. Why did you get me something that you knew I'd hate?* But I just said, "Well, I'm not sure if I'll like it all that much."

"No, pet, course you aren't sure. That's because you've never tried it. But I've got a good feeling about it!"

"Granny used to do ballet, you know," Mum said, as though that would make it better. *Ha ha.*

The thought of having to go to ballet lessons was bad enough, because everyone knows I'm the tomboy sort of girl and not the ballet sort, so, for a start, my brothers would tease me more than ever. But, to make matters worse, Granny had specially booked me in at the strictest ballet school for miles around – the Coralie Charlton School of Ballet.

She'd given me another present, too. It was one of those little Russian dolls, made of brightly painted wood, that you pull apart in the middle and you find another doll inside, and then another inside that one, and a really teensy one on the very inside.

"It's lovely, isn't it?" said Mum with worried eyes. (She knew how I felt about dolls, you see.) But, actually, she didn't have to worry because I thought it was wicked, and I couldn't stop taking all the little dolls out and putting them back in again.

"The doll reminds me of you," Granny had said, twinkling, "because she's got a lot more inside her than she thinks she has!" Then she'd started chuckling again.

I hadn't got the faintest idea what Granny was on about, but I gave her a big grin anyway, and thanked her again.

When I'd done quite a few weeks at ballet and I didn't hate it any more, Granny started asking me to show her all the steps. At first, I didn't want to because I wasn't much good at it, and I thought Granny might get bored watching and think she'd wasted her money on me. But she went into a smiley daydream when I was doing the exercises and said, "I could watch you all day, pet." And that made me feel as though I was better than I really was.

I love it when Granny comes round now, because she's the only person in my family who's interested in ballet. Mum's always too busy and Dad thinks it's a waste of space, and my brothers just tease me about it and call me a *twirly girly* and things like that. But Granny can even remember the names of the steps from when she was a girl. We usually go up to my room, and while I'm getting changed into my leotard, she looks at all my gym trophies and sometimes gives them a polish. Granny knows where I won every single one of them because she always comes with Mum and Dad to watch when I do competitions. I'm so lucky having the granny that I've got.

"You're arching your back, Rose."

Miss Coralie's voice made me jump. She was

frowning at me, so I quickly corrected myself and she gave me one of her *that'll-do* nods. I sighed without letting it show. We were more than halfway through the lesson and I hadn't even got a *nice* let alone a *lovely*. That was gym's fault. But what am I supposed to do? I love gym and I want to do well in the competition. That's why I've got to practise so hard.

I sighed again. Pleasing Miss Coralie *and* my gym teacher was impossible.

2 Not Enough Oomph

It was Wednesday morning break. Poppy was waiting for me right by the year-five door. Her face broke into a big smile when I came into the playground.

"Hi! I thought you might have got kept in again."

I grinned at her. "Don't worry, I was just finishing my apple."

"So, tell me what happened in your lesson."

After my ballet class, Miss Coralie teaches grade five, so I always see Jasmine and Poppy lining up in the corridor when I'm going back into the changing room. There's no time to talk, and anyway their line is supposed to be silent, but they always do questioning eyebrows to find out if I got a *lovely* or not. (They know I'm dying for Miss Coralie to say that magic word to me.) Yesterday after class, I shook my head to show them that I hadn't got one, same as usual, and they both looked disappointed, same as usual, but then I wrinkled my nose as well, which was my way of telling them that it had been worse than that.

"It was just that Miss Coralie corrected me more than usual."

Poppy put her arm round me and didn't say anything for a moment. I knew why. It was because she was trying to think of something kind to say. "Never mind. It's only because she thinks you're good and she wants you to get better."

"I think she's fed up with always having to say the same things to me."

Poppy looked a bit anxious then. "Is it because you keep standing like a gymnast?"

I nodded. "It must be because I'm doing so much extra gym at the moment, and it's getting me into the habit of arching my back and straightening my arms too much and all that kind of stuff. It never used to matter before I started ballet."

"Do you think Miss Coralie minds?"

I shrugged. "Dunno. I just have to keep saying, 'Come on brain, remember it's ballet today.' And then when I'm at gym practice, 'Forget about ballet, brain, it's gym today!'"

"Oh, well. It won't be for long," said Poppy, grabbing my hand. "Come on, I'll help you with *jetés.*"

Poppy and Jasmine are dying for my gym competition to be over because they both know I'll never be in their ballet class with them until I've passed grade four. And that's not going to happen until I stop getting ballet mixed up with gym.

Not Enough Oomph

We'd only just started on the *jetés* when Miss Banner, the gym teacher, appeared at the playground gate, with her portable CD player in one hand and her bag in the other.

Poppy gave me a bit of an accusing look, as though I'd specially invited Miss Banner today. "*She* doesn't usually come on Wednesdays!"

"Extra practice." I sighed.

"But that'll make three times this week!" squeaked Poppy.

"Four, actually."

"Four! But you only do ballet *once*! It's no wonder you keep over arching and everything." Poppy had gone a bit pink. She'd probably just realized how stressy she was sounding.

Miss Banner spotted me and came jogging over. "Make sure you're in the hall at one o'clock prompt, Rose. And can you tell Sasha and Katie?"

There must have been a bit of fed-upness still left on my face because Miss Banner was just turning to go when she suddenly gave me a teachery look. "Gymnasts don't get anywhere without hard work, you know, Rose. Anyway, I thought you loved your gym..."

I wasn't sure what to say to that and decided it might be best to keep quiet in case something came out that sounded cheeky by mistake. Sometimes it's hard to judge the right things to say to teachers. At least, it is for *me*.

"Good, Rose... And get ready for your run up..."

The energy came swishing up my legs and zooming into my top half. Miss Banner watched me as I set off towards the vault like a plane going down a runway, getting faster and faster. I bounced off the springboard and slapped my hands onto the middle of the vault, felt my legs fling up as my back arched and I flew into my handspring. A second later, I was on the crash mattress, feet together, legs stretched, back arched even more, and my head flung back.

Not Enough Oomph

"Lovely presentation at the end there, Rose, and nice flight off and landing, but the attack to the vault was a bit weak, and that's because you're not giving it enough oomph. You've got to forget about being gentle and balletic and really go for it."

Not enough oomph? How much oomph did she want? "I ran as hard as I could...I thought I was the oomphiest person on the planet, to be honest."

Miss Banner was glaring at me as though I'd just said *big bums* or something. "But you were running like a ballet dancer, far too high up on the balls of your feet. I don't know how I'm going to get you out of the habit..." She didn't even finish her sentence, just shook her head and then turned to Sasha and Katie, who were both looking at the floor.

"Right, let's go through the floor-work routine to finish."

We all went to our starting positions on the

thin mats and Miss Banner watched the three of us carefully as we stayed still as statues.

"Lovely, Sasha... Can you drop your head a bit more, Katie...?" She pointed the remote at the CD player and the music started. "And *five* and *six* and *seven* and *eight* and..."

It was a three-minute routine and we know it really well because we've practised it so much. I felt strong and full of energy as I went in and out of rolls and springs, twists and jumps, balances and stretches. Miss Banner didn't say a word until the music had finished and we were holding our final shapes.

"Great! It's really coming on." She turned to me with a smile that was trying to make up for the telling off. "This is where ballet can be helpful, and you've certainly got a lovely dance quality to your floor work now, but your arms are rather curvy and soft. I just wish I could sharpen you up a bit..." She suddenly stood up straight in the middle of the mat, her arms in ballet fifth position. "Look, Rose." She purposely bent her elbows too much and drooped her wrists so her fingers dangled. "That's ballet!" Then she straightened her arms into a wide straight V-shape with fingers neatly together. "And *that's* gym!"

I tried to keep my face blank even though I really would have liked to stick my tongue out at her. I hate it when teachers exaggerate, especially as you aren't allowed to argue with them and you just have to wait until they've finished.

"One more time through, then we'll call it a day, girls."

This time I concentrated hard and when it got to the middle bit I stretched my arms like mad.

"Miles better!" said Miss Banner at the end. Her eyes were all sparkly.

"Well done," whispered Katie, as she and Sasha rushed off to get changed.

I was about to follow them but Miss Banner called me over.

"I've had details today about a big competition later in the year for solo entries and I'd like to enter you, Rose." She patted my shoulder. "It'll take extra training, but I'll have a word with your mum about my Saturday-afternoon class."

Lots of jumbled thoughts whizzed around my head.

Miss Banner has chosen me to compete in a big competition. Yesss! – But I'd have to go to gym class on Saturday afternoons when I really want to be with Jasmine and Poppy. – I'd get better and better at gym and make everyone really proud of me. – Yes, but I'd get worse and worse at ballet. – No, I could try harder and harder at ballet. – But Miss Coralie would still be able to tell I was doing lots of gym. She's already noticed. She'd say that gym and ballet don't mix. – I've found that out already. – I'd have to give one of them up. – I don't want to. – I'd have to. – I don't want to. – I'd...

None of the thoughts would stay still for long enough to turn into a proper sentence that I could actually say to Miss Banner. But she was waiting for me to say *something*. Her eyes were staring so hard that I began to think she might have some special powers to see inside my head and any second now she'd tell me off for wanting to do ballet just as much as I wanted to do gym. Then, suddenly, her whole face turned into a smile and she said, "One thing at a time, though. Let's get *this* competition over with first, shall we?"

I nodded, feeling relieved that I didn't have to speak after all. All I wanted was to get back to Poppy. With a bit of luck there might still be a few minutes of break before the bell for afternoon school. "See you tomorrow, Miss Banner."

"See you tomorrow, Rose." I was almost out

of the door when she added, "And don't forget to bring plenty of *oomph* with you!"

I gulped. I wished there was no such word as *oomph*. In fact, I wished there was no such word as competition. I used to love them... But I don't know what's the matter with me now.

3 Granny

On Sunday, Granny came round for lunch. She wanted to know all the details about the gym competition.

"A very important date for my diary, pet!"

Then Mum said lunch wouldn't be ready for twenty minutes, so I grabbed Granny's hand.

"Do you want to watch me doing ballet, or shall we go outside and I'll show you some of the floor work for the gym competition?"

"Now, you be careful, Rose," said Mum, waving a cloth at me from the kitchen door. "Don't do anything that might strain your muscles, or you'll have Miss Banner up in arms."

"It'll be okay as long as I don't do handsprings and stuff."

"Probably better not to take any risks as you've got the competition coming up," said Granny, patting my hand. "Come on, let's go to your room."

I was already wearing my ballet leotard because Poppy and Jazz were coming round after lunch. They were going to help me with the set variations. I couldn't wait.

"It's taking you a long time to grow into this leotard of yours, isn't it?" said Granny as we reached the top of the stairs.

"I reckon it'd fit *you*, Gran!" said my brother, Adam, suddenly appearing in his bedroom doorway.

"Too much cheek by far, for an eleven year old!" joked Granny.

Adam just grinned and whizzed downstairs. Granny never does proper tellings off.

※

At lunch time, Dad told everyone what Miss Banner had said when she phoned about the big competition.

He winked at me and I felt quite proud. "She thinks you're the bee's knees!"

Mum suddenly started flapping her hand in the air. "Yes! And I forgot to tell you, Rose, Miss Banner wants you to do more classes. She's not even going to charge us, and she says she's going to work out a daily practice routine for you centred around body conditioning!" She leaned forwards with sparkling eyes. "What do you think of *that*, then?"

It was happening again. The thoughts were whizzing around inside my head but none of them would stay still. So I just shrugged, and said, "Dunno."

"I thought you'd be over the moon," said Mum, frowning. "Miss Banner sounded very excited, you know."

I stabbed a piece of pork chop and skated it round my plate on the end of my fork. "She gets cross sometimes."

"What for?" said Jack. (He's fifteen, by the way.)

"When I get confused with ballet..."

"You ought to give up ballet. It's for wusses," said Rory, my thirteen-year-old brother.

"Don't speak with your mouth full," said Mum. She was staring at the peas really hard, then she suddenly gave me a gentle look. "You can always give up ballet until the gym competition's over if you want, love."

But that wasn't what I wanted. "No, I don't want to miss any ballet. Except..."

Granny tipped her head on one side. "What's up, pet?"

"It's just that Miss Coralie gets a bit fed up, too. She says I keep dancing like a gymnast."

Dad started stabbing the air with his fork.

Granny

"Somebody ought to tell Miss Coralie that the reason you dance like a gymnast is because you *are* one!"

I didn't like to hear Dad getting cross with Miss Coralie. He didn't understand. "She's only telling the truth, Dad. If you do loads of gym it really *is* bad for ballet, honestly."

"What rubbish," said Dad, leaning back in his chair and folding his arms.

"Why don't you give up gym then?" said Adam. "Can I have some more chips, Mum?"

Mum nodded. "Rose wouldn't dream of giving up gym, would you, Rose?" She didn't wait for an answer. "Miss Banner said she's the best in the school at it. And you can't go giving up something when you've got a real talent for it, can you?"

"How come *ballet's* bad for *gym*?" asked Jack.

"Just is," I said, remembering how Miss Banner had stood in the middle of the mats with dangly arms.

"So give up ballet, like I said. *Dur!*" said Rory.

Suddenly, I'd had enough of the whole conversation. Everyone thought they knew all the answers, but there weren't any answers. I just wished they'd all shut up. "Can I get down please, Mum?"

"You've not had any pudding, love."

"I'm not really hungry."

"Go on, then." I could feel her eyes on me as I went towards the kitchen.

"Going to practise ballet, I bet," called Adam. Then he put on the posh voice he uses when he's pretending to be my ballet teacher. "Point those toes, now Rosie Pose!"

Everyone laughed. At least, I think they did. I didn't stop to check, just ran down the back steps and onto the lawn. The grass was a bit damp, but that never bothers me. I kicked off my trainers, pulled off my socks, put my hand on the side of the old swing and started doing *pliés*. I could hear the *plié* music in my head, almost as though Mrs. Marsden was playing it. But when I went on to *battements tendus*, I couldn't remember the music at all, so my head started filling up with the conversation we'd just had. It made me mad that everyone seemed to think that ballet wasn't anything important. They ought to go to lessons, then they'd find out.

"That's a fierce face!" I looked sideways and saw Granny coming down the back steps. I was glad it was her and not anyone else in my smelly family. "Sorry, pet. I didn't mean to interrupt your *battements tendus*. I just thought you looked a bit fed up when you came out here."

"I hate it when everyone says stuff about ballet."

Granny sat on the swing and started swinging gently to and fro. I noticed how straight her back was. And when she stretched her legs out at the front, they were straight too. I don't think many grannies would have such lovely, strong, upright bodies as that. Most ladies go a bit humpy and lumpy when they get old. "They don't understand how much you like it, pet. I should just ignore them."

"But I can't ignore Miss Coralie and Miss Banner, can I? I'm fed up with getting told off when it's not my fault."

"They're not exactly telling you off, are they? Just trying to make you better at the thing they teach."

I didn't know what to say after that, because Granny was right, but it still left a ginormous problem inside my head. I stared at the ground and found my foot doing *ronds de jambe* without me telling it to.

"When I was your age," Granny started to say, in a slow daydreamy voice, "I felt as though I could see my whole life ahead of me, like a long, straight, smooth-flowing river..." She was looking at the sky with an almost-smile on her face. I stopped doing *ronds de jambe* so I could listen better, because I had the feeling Granny was about to tell me something important. A very thoughtful look came over her face. "It wasn't till I was seventeen that I realized something about rivers, though. You see..." She stopped right in the middle of her sentence because we'd both heard a loud knocking on the window. I looked up to see Dad mouthing that Poppy and Jasmine were here.

"Ooh, lovely. Now you can all get dancing together!" said Granny.

"They're going to teach me the grade four set variations!"

"That'll be good. You'll have to show me afterwards."

Then Poppy and Jasmine were standing at the back door, Jasmine in third position and Poppy with her head tilted, which made her neck look really graceful.

"Go and dance your heart out!" called Granny as I rushed off.

But the moment we were up in my room, I burst into a flood of talking and talking about Miss Banner and Miss Coralie and how impossible it was to be a gymnast *and* do ballet.

"Miss Banner must think you're brilliant, Rose!" said Jasmine, when I was in the middle of the bit about all the extra gym practices. "She might be thinking that you could represent the country one day! Think how good that would be!"

"But I'd have to give up ballet!" I said in a bit of a squeak, because I couldn't believe that Jasmine seemed to be agreeing with Mum and Dad, when I thought she was my ballet friend.

"I'm sure it'll be all right to carry on doing both…" said Poppy. "I can't wait to see you in the competition."

"I can't wait to see *myself*!" I said, which made them both burst out laughing. "But what's going to happen afterwards? I mean, just imagine if we couldn't get together on Saturday afternoons because I had to do more gym practice!"

"We'd just have to do ballet on Sundays instead – like right now!" said Poppy.

They were both talking as though it was no problem at all, but there was something not quite right. And then I realized what it was. Their eyes seemed worried and they wouldn't look at me. So what was I supposed to believe, their eyes or their voices? And will someone please tell me why there are so many unanswered questions racing around inside my head these days?

"Come on, let's get on with it!" said Jasmine. "I'll be Miss Coralie..." She'd already taken off her leggings and top and was wearing her leotard underneath. "Good afternoon, girls..." Poppy quickly took her jeans off so she was ready too, and stood by my windowsill, which we use for a *barre*.

Any second now Jasmine would say, "First

position and prepare the arm to second..." just like Miss Coralie does, so I quickly rushed over to my desk and sat down.

"Rose! What are you doing!" said Jasmine, forgetting who she was supposed to be for a moment.

"I'm being Mrs. Marsden," I told her. "I mean, *someone's* got to be the pianist, haven't they?"

Poppy was laughing too much to stand up straight. "You're mad, Rose!"

And she was right, I *am* a bit mad. But these days, it's only the top layer. Underneath, I'm deadly serious and all confused. Especially now my best friends don't even know the answer to my problem.

4 Time to Make a Decision

It wasn't until I was lying in bed that night that I remembered how Granny had been just about to tell me something when Poppy and Jasmine had arrived. It had sounded as though it was going to be important and suddenly I just *had* to know what it was that Granny had found out when she was seventeen. I don't know why, but I thought it might help me sort things out in my own life.

The first thing I did the next morning was ask Mum if I could go round to Granny's after school, but she told me that Granny was going to stay with Uncle Rupert until Thursday. I felt a bit sad about that. Thursday was three whole days away.

Monday night's homework was horrible and I didn't really get what it was on about so I asked if I could phone Jazz. She'd be sure to know the answers. But first she wanted to know how the gym class had gone.

I told her it was okay – "Well, the second half was. For the first half, Miss Banner told me I was too dreamy."

A big gasp came down the line. "*You! Dreamy!*"

"I know!"

"Perhaps she meant *day*dreamy, not the gentle floaty sort of dreamy."

"No, she definitely meant the gentle floaty sort. It made me really mad so after that I turned into the opposite of dreamy and went all hard and sharp."

There was a silence when I said that. I knew

what Jazz was thinking — that she didn't want me to be *too* hard and sharp or Miss Coralie would get cross with me. I couldn't be bothered to go through all that again so I asked her about the homework and by the time we'd finished I had to get off the phone because Dad said I'd been on long enough.

After I'd done the homework I started thinking about ballet, and I felt really determined to get a *lovely* in the lesson the next day. So I decided to get every bit of gym right out of my body by shaking myself hard, and kicking my feet. But after only about a minute Dad came up and said that the ceiling was trembling in the sitting room, and that whatever I was doing had to stop.

All through Tuesday at school I got more and more nervous – the excited sort of nervous – and by the time we all ran in at the start of Miss Coralie's lesson, and found our places on the *barre*, I couldn't wait to get started. Miss

Coralie didn't really notice my *pliés* because she was correcting some of the girls at the other end of the *barre*, but when it came to *ronds de jambe* she was standing right next to me.

"Your placing's gone completely haywire, Rose. Lower that hip."

She might as well have poked me in the stomach and said *I hate you*, the way she made me feel at that moment. I'd been so sure I was all lined up properly. I lowered my hip as carefully as I could, but I could still feel my leg turning in.

"Dear, oh dear!" She bent down and altered my leg and foot. "What's happened to your turnout?" She straightened up. "That's better... But I shouldn't have to remind you every five minutes." I was cross with myself then, because I should have realized my placing was wrong.

I concentrated as hard as I could right to the end of the *barre* work, and all that time I could feel Miss Coralie's eyes on me. Then we moved to the centre and still her eyes seemed to be on me more than on anyone else. We were right in the middle of the *port de bras* when she suddenly said, "Arms, Rose!" I quickly snapped them into a strong, straight V and arched my back at the same time.

Why had one of the girls behind me gasped? And why was Miss Coralie looking so stern? Then I realized where I was. At ballet. Not gym. Oh, no! My arms immediately bent like thin branches snapping, as my heart somersaulted down to my stomach.

"What *are* you doing, Rose?"

"Sorry, I was getting confused."

The music for the exercise had finished now and it seemed very quiet. Mrs. Marsden was looking down at her hands in her lap. The girls in the row in front had all turned round to stare at me. If I'd been anywhere but here I would have pulled a face and asked them if they wanted a picture. But I just stood there, keeping my face blank.

"Let's move on to the *adage*, girls."

And that was it. Everyone faced the right way for the next exercise, Mrs. Marsden's eyes were on her music, my heart went back into its place and the lesson carried on as normal. But I didn't enjoy it one bit because I had to keep giving myself instructions all the time, like: *Bend your arms, Rose! Don't arch your back, Rose! Turn OUT, Rose! Don't be so sharp, Rose!* It was a relief when we got to the *révérence*. Then, I was about to go out to the changing room with everyone else when Miss Coralie called me back.

"Rose, I want a word about gym. Are you doing more than usual at the moment?"

"Well, yes, there's another competition, you see... But it'll soon be over."

She gave me one of her half-smiles. I felt as though I'd scored five out of ten with that answer. Then I couldn't help watching her lips to see what score I'd get for the next one.

"I see. So when the competition's over, you'll be going back to what? A weekly gym lesson?"

The trouble was, Mum was really keen for me to do the Saturday afternoon class. "Erm...I'm not really sure..."

Well *that* scored me about two, I guess.

"You love your gym, don't you?"

Easy question. I nodded and waited for her lips to move, but they didn't. Her eyes had turned even more serious, with a bit of sadness in them. "You're lovely and flexible, Rose, and that's probably largely because of all your gym... I should imagine you're a very talented gymnast, and it's no wonder your teacher is keen for you to enter competitions and get plenty of practice and so on... But all the time you're doing *this* amount of gym, you're not going to get anywhere with ballet. It affects your placing so much..." Her eyes had got softness in them now, which was spreading all over her face. I'd never ever seen that before in Miss Coralie. "When you first started ballet I didn't realize you'd be doing *so* much gym, or I'd have explained that the two don't really mix. Maybe it's time to make a decision about whether you're going to concentrate on ballet or gym."

There was a long pause. I suppose we'd come to the end of the conversation. I didn't know what the right answer was, so I just stood there.

"Go away and have a think about it. Talk to your parents. Ask them to phone me if they want. I'll be very happy to discuss it with them."

Her smile grew the teeniest bit bigger, but it was only to get rid of me. So I nodded and ran out of the room as she called out, "Come in, class."

Poppy and Jasmine were giving me big-eyed looks from the line.

"What?" asked Jasmine in a squeaky whisper.

I shook my head because there wasn't time to

talk, and they both came out of the line to press their thumbs against mine. We call it a thumb-thumb and it's usually for luck, but this time it was just because they felt sorry for me.

"I'll phone you later," I said.

But I didn't really know what good it would do, because Poppy and Jasmine don't do gym. How could they possibly understand that if I gave it up I'd be giving up half my life, and if I gave up ballet, I'd be giving up the other half?

5 The Wrong Kind of Audience

In the car on the way home I kept on *nearly* telling Mum what Miss Coralie had said. But I couldn't think of the right words because I knew Mum would get a bit cross and say that she didn't see why I shouldn't carry on with both. Then *I'd* get a bit cross trying to explain that they don't mix properly. And that would be the end of that.

If I talked to Dad about it, he'd probably just tell me to give up ballet. And I didn't want to. I couldn't ask any of my brothers what they thought I should do because they weren't properly interested in anything I did. Poppy and Jasmine would both want to me to give up gym, only they'd be too nice to say that, because they know I love it. So there was no one left for me to talk to except Granny, and she wouldn't be back till Thursday.

While Mum made the tea, I sat at the kitchen table reading my *World of Ballet* book. Really, I was only turning the pages and looking at the pictures. It was just that I wanted to be in the same room as Mum in case I suddenly found the right words to explain about ballet and gym, because I'd worked out that it was going to be forty-eight whole hours before I could see Granny, and that was a very long time. Anyway, it was cosy in the kitchen.

But then Adam came in and spoiled it. "Rory's nicked my football socks. He says they're his, but they're not, are they, Mum?"

Mum yanked open the tumble dryer, pulled out a pair of socks and threw them to Adam.

"There you go. Sort it out between yourselves."

Adam caught them, then looked at me. "What are you doing?"

"Nothing."

"Why are you all quiet?"

"I'm not."

"What are you reading?" He looked at the cover and put on his sneery voice. "*World of Ballet*. Has it got Miss Coronary in it?" He sniggered.

"*Coralie!*" I snapped.

"When's tea, Mum?"

"Fifteen minutes."

"Can I have a biscuit?"

"No."

"A raisin?"

"Go on, then."

Adam helped himself to a handful of raisins and came and sat at the table with me to eat them. I put the book up to hide his face from my view. Then he stood up and started to imitate the dancer on the front cover who was in an *arabesque*. "Is this right?"

I snapped the book shut, trying hard to keep my crossness inside me, and said I was going outside.

"To dance on your tippy toes," said Adam in a whisper so Mum wouldn't hear.

"No, gym actually!" I only said that because Adam thinks I'm quite clever to be able to do half the gym things I do.

"Bet you're not doing gym," he said.

I didn't bother to answer him, just went out. As I was shutting the door behind me, I heard Mum telling him off for teasing me. At least I knew then that it would be safe to do ballet, even though it was right outside the kitchen window, because Mum would stop Adam watching me. It had been raining and the grass was a bit wet, but I still took my socks and trainers off so I could point my toes properly.

As I slowly practised my *ronds de jambe*, I found myself filling up with another load of determination to get a *lovely* from Miss Coralie, even though it was only about an hour since I'd been thinking it would be impossible *ever* to get one. I tried to imagine Miss Coralie's eyes on me, and made myself keep my hips square. I couldn't stop my working leg turning in when I slid my toe round to the back, though.

Suddenly there was a knock on an upstairs window and, like an idiot, I looked up. Adam opened Rory's window, stuck his leg on the windowsill and then put his arms above his head rather like Miss Banner had done.

I should have just ignored him and carried on, but it's hard doing ballet practice with anyone watching because it's private. It's got feelings in it and you have to make the feelings come out. That's fine when I'm in a class with *everyone* showing their feelings, but you feel a bit stupid when you're the only one. It would be much easier to just pretend I was doing exercises for gym. So I quickly changed from *ronds de jambe* to the sideways splits.

"Doesn't that hurt?" asked Rory, appearing next to Adam at the window.

I felt quite clever having both of them watching me and knowing that neither of them could do anything like that, so I did a handstand and walked a few steps. But it made me feel guilty because of doing something I wasn't supposed to do. Miss Banner was always giving us lectures about practising at home and how easy it is to strain wrists and ankles, so I came down from the handstand.

"Hey, she's good, your sister!"

I looked up at the sound of the strange voice to see one of Rory's friends at the window.

"Show us one of those round-off things," said Rory.

"I'm not really allowed," I said, shrugging my shoulders to show it wasn't me who made up the rules. "I could twist my ankle or something. And I've got the competition…"

"Anyway, what *is* a round-off?" asked Rory's friend.

"Just do one, Ro…to show Jonno. Go on… You're really good at them."

It was such a lovely feeling hearing Rory saying nice things when I'm used to nothing but teasing, but still I wasn't sure.

"It'll be good practice for the competition," said Jonno.

He was right. It would. And just one wouldn't do any harm, would it? So I went to the top of the garden to get the longest possible run up.

But then Adam suddenly spoke in his I-know-best voice. "You're supposed to warm up first, you know."

"I *am* warmed up," I told him. I couldn't help snapping because I'd been just about to start and he'd interrupted my concentration.

"Well, don't blame me if you get injured," he

said, making his voice go all grown-up and clever.

I glanced at the kitchen window to check Mum wasn't watching. There was no sign of her, so I set off, pounding the ground with my hard steps. It felt easy because it was slightly downhill, and when I sprung off my hands, my legs flung over really fast and the ground seemed to come up to meet my feet before I was expecting it. I had to do a little jump to stop myself crashing forwards. And it was then that I felt a pain like a hot knife cutting into the top of my right foot.

6 Dreading the Next Day

Rory and Jonno both whistled and whooped as they turned away. Adam was the only one there now. I could feel his eyes on me. My foot was in agony but there was no way I was going to let smarty pants know that. I carefully sat down on the ground, put my legs in a wide V and did some stretches over my legs. My foot didn't hurt in this position, thank goodness, so I knew I could carry on doing them for as long as I wanted.

"You've hurt yourself, haven't you?" came Adam's I'm-so-clever voice. "I can tell. It's because you didn't warm up properly, isn't it?"

How could he tell, the big pooh? And anyway it wasn't because of not warming up properly, it was because of the ground sloping.

"I haven't hurt myself at all. I don't know what you're talking about," I told him.

I was wishing I hadn't sat down, because that meant I had to stand up again, and I knew it was going to hurt. Maybe if I tried kneeling first. So I carefully got on to my knees without putting any pressure on my foot, and started doing some sideways stretches.

Hurry up and go, Adam!

"If it doesn't hurt, let's see you stand up, then!" he said, all sneery.

"I will...when I've done this." And I changed to head rolls so I could keep an eye on the upstairs window. Every time I looked, the big know-all was still there. It was obvious he was waiting to catch me out, and if I did even the teensiest wince he'd say, *See! Told you! You* have *injured yourself!*

And it was right at that moment that it hit me. *I HAD injured myself.* I might not be able to do the competition. After all that work, I'd be letting everyone down. Especially me. And as for Miss Banner, she'd go absolutely mad. And so would Miss Coralie. *And* Mum and Dad. But why was I thinking about Adam? Who cared about Adam? Except that if he saw me limping he'd probably tell Mum straight away, and then the whole big horrible telling off would start. I felt awful. All I wanted was to be on my own so I could wiggle my foot around and try rubbing it and see how bad it was. But I couldn't do anything except silly head rolls because of hawk eyes watching me all the time.

If only I hadn't been such a show-off. No wonder Miss Banner doesn't like people trying out their skills at home. Anyway, I couldn't do head rolls for ever. I had to stand up. Okay... slowly and carefully...

"See! Your ankle's hurting, isn't it?"

I didn't have to tell a lie. It was nothing to do with my ankle. "No it's not, know-all! I'm just going slowly because that's what you're supposed to do. It's all part of the stretching."

I put my weight on my right foot. It *did* hurt, but it wasn't agony. I could easily pretend it was perfectly all right just till I got back inside the house.

Adam was pointing at me by now. "You're faking it! I'll tell Mum. She'll know what to do."

He was just trying to catch me out. He wanted me to say: *No, please don't tell!*

But all I said was "I'm Okay, *okay?*"

"Do a handstand, then. You're allowed to do ordinary handstands, aren't you?"

So I did, and as I came down I felt that same stabbing pain, but I managed not to flinch or anything, just stood there, looking up. "There! Satisfied?"

"You were lucky," was all he said. Then he shut the window with a loud click.

The moment he was gone I put my socks and trainers back on. Then, when I was quite sure no one was watching from any of the windows, I tested out my right foot by walking slowly towards the back door. If I stepped very gently, and took care that my foot was facing exactly forwards, it didn't hurt at all, but if I put it down quickly and it was pointing even a tiny bit in the wrong direction it really hurt.

By the time I got to the back door I was beginning to worry about how I was going to hide it from everyone. The whole family was used to seeing me darting about all over the place. They'd know something was wrong if I suddenly started going around like an ancient tortoise.

And when I thought about gym practice the next day...I just had to shake the thought away because I had absolutely no idea what in the world I was going to say to Miss Banner. All I knew was that it wouldn't be the truth or she'd kill me.

"Tea's ready." Luckily, Mum wasn't looking at me, she was stirring something in a pan. "Can you go and wash your hands, Rose, and tell the boys to come down and set the table?"

I walked slowly across the kitchen and had nearly reached the hall door when Mum said, "What's the matter with your foot?"

"Nothing. It's just...a floor exercise Miss Banner said I ought to do. You walk very slowly and try to let every bit of your foot spread out. But it's important that you keep your feet pointing exactly forwards."

I don't know where on earth my brain managed to find that answer, but it sounded just like the truth.

"Uh-huh..." said Mum in the murmury voice that meant she was concentrating on something completely different. Then she suddenly went bright and brisk again. "Oh, Granny phoned and she's coming back tomorrow instead of Thursday."

A big zing of happiness went right through my body. At last something good had happened. "Can I go round and see her after school then?"

"I expect so." Mum smiled.

I smiled too. Only one more day, then Granny would talk to me in her lovely granny voice and help me sort out all the jumble inside my head. And she'd never be cross with me for getting an injury.

But right in the middle of my lovely thoughts the big shivery thought came back. Before I saw Granny, I had to get through school. It was going to be like a terrible nightmare. Just a horrible day of faking and pretending and lying. Unless, by some miracle, my foot got better overnight. I knew that resting injured bits of your body does them good. Right, I'd hop everywhere as long as no one was watching, then I'd go to bed early so it could rest for the longest possible time.

I sighed as I turned round to go upstairs on my bottom. Somehow, I didn't think it was going to work. If only Poppy and Jasmine were here to do a thumb-thumb...

7 Everything Coming to the Surface

"What am I going to do, Poppy?" I asked her for the trillionth time.

"Just try wiggling it. See if it's got any better in the last five minutes. It might have done, you never know."

"I spent ages wiggling it in bed last night, and that didn't do any good, so I don't think it's going to make much difference now."

A thoughtful look came over Poppy's face and she spoke slowly, staring at the far wall of the playground. "Perhaps you ought to tell Miss Banner the truth."

"What! You're joking!"

"No, listen. Miss Banner might know which cream you're supposed to put on it...or some special exercises that you can do...or something."

"It's a good idea, Poppy, except that I really don't want to get killed for breaking the rules. I'm too young to die."

Poppy wasn't in the mood for my jokes. Neither was *I* really. "No, you don't have to tell the *whole* truth. You could say you did it falling downstairs or you tripped over."

I shook my head. "Miss Banner knows everything about muscles and all those little – what d'you call them – ligaments and things. She'd guess I was lying because it's probably impossible to get an injury on the top of your foot from falling downstairs."

"So what *are* you going to do then?"

While Poppy had been talking about falling downstairs, a plan had been coming into my brain.

I spoke slowly to test it out. "What if...I pretended...to be...ill?"

"They'd send you home, and your mum'd know straight away that you weren't really!" Poppy said in a rush.

"Okay, not ill...more....kind of tired..."

Poppy didn't say anything, so I told her to put her arm round me, then I made my shoulders go all droopy. "Try to look as though you're worried about me."

And sure enough, when we'd stayed like that for a minute or two, the teacher came over.

"Are you all right, Rose?"

"I feel a bit funny – kind of tired..."

And by one o'clock, all the teachers, including Miss Banner, thought it was best not to exhaust me by making me do gym practice.

"Better to miss one practice and get yourself back on form," said Miss Banner, tilting my chin back to look closely at me. It reminded me of when Mum searches Jack's face for blackheads.

"Let's see how you are tomorrow. I'm sure you'll be fine."

I nodded and tried to make sure I kept my droopy look in place. Then I walked slowly away, being careful to take only footsteps that faced forwards.

A little voice inside me was whispering, *What if it isn't better by tomorrow? Or even worse, what if it isn't better in time for the competition?* But I decided to ignore that voice and just hope for the best.

At the end of school, Mrs. Henderson, my class teacher, had a word with Mum and explained about me being tired.

"Tired? Well she's not short of sleep..." said Mum.

"No, I think it's just all the gym practice that's suddenly got on top of her. It's understandable."

Mum was frowning at me as though she didn't think it was at all understandable. I leaned my head into her and she put her arm round me, looking totally puzzled. "Come on then, love. Let's get you home."

Then I wished I hadn't leaned into her because now I had to get out from under her arm. Otherwise, I wouldn't be able to walk with my feet facing properly forwards and it still hurt like mad when I put my right foot down wrongly.

"I *can* still go to Granny's, can't I?" I asked, the moment we set off.

"So you don't feel too tired to go to Granny's?" She didn't exactly sound cross, just puzzled.

"It's not tiring at Granny's. We just talk."

Mum looked as though she was thinking hard, but then all the thoughts came pouring out in a rush.

"You see, I'm not sure what's wrong with you, Rose. I've never known you feel tired for no reason before. I mean...what kind of tiredness is it? Do your eyes feel sleepy? Or does your body feel tired, or what?"

I knew I had to be careful. The teachers had believed me completely but it wasn't so easy to fool Mum. "Body," I said.

She seemed to ignore that. "Or is there a reason why you didn't want to go to gym? Because if there is, you only have to tell me, love."

She turned her head sideways and the look on her face reminded me of when I was only about five and I'd eaten some ice cream straight from the tub in the freezer without asking, and Mum was trying to get me to admit it.

"I just felt too tired to do all those hard things again," I said, doing a big sigh.

Mum patted my knee and we drove the rest of the way with a thoughtful silence around us.

At six-thirty, I was sitting in the big armchair at Granny's, which has got its own special smell. I was balancing a plate of biscuits on my lap. Well, to be precise, I was whizzing them round to see how fast they'd spin without falling off, because they were very thin shiny ones that slid about. Granny said she'd got them from Uncle Rupert.

"Did you have a nice time at Great Uncle Rupert's?"

"Wonderful! We've been reminiscing."

"What's that?"

"Talking about the old days...and looking at photos from when we were both young."

"Ooh, can I look? Are there any of when you used to do ballet?"

She pointed towards the sideboard. "Fetch me over those albums, pet. I got them out just before you came."

I remembered to walk carefully.

"Dearie me, what have you done to your foot?"

I couldn't help a bit of a gasp coming out.

"How did you know?"

"Because I know my granddaughter, and she doesn't walk like a snail unless there's something wrong with her." She gave another chuckle. "Show me which bit it is, and I'll see what I can do!"

I put the albums on the coffee table, then sat down with my foot on Granny's lap. "It's just here." I pressed the place, which was in a fleshy hollow bit on top but not quite in the middle. "Ouch!"

"Yes, I see..." She lent forwards and touched it herself. "Does that hurt?"

I nodded.

"How did you do it?"

I told her the truth right away and she wasn't at all cross. Just said, "That'll be a tendon. We'll see what we can do with that."

But, as Granny started to massage my foot, I noticed what it said on the front cover of the photograph album: *Me — 14 to 17*. Then I spotted something else right at the bottom of the cover. Someone had cut out a picture of a ballet shoe and stuck it in the corner.

"Are these photos of you doing ballet, Granny? Did you do it until you were seventeen? I didn't know that!" I sat up and took my foot off her lap. Then I realized Granny wasn't answering. I turned to look at her. She was smiling with twinkling secretive eyes. And suddenly I knew...I snatched up the album and turned to the first page. Then I gasped and held my breath as I stared and stared at the beautiful photo.

She was wearing a leotard and a little ballet skirt, standing on *pointe*, in the most perfect *arabesque*, like a real ballerina.

"Wow! You were amazing!" I breathed.

And when I looked up, I saw that Granny had tears in her eyes.

8 The River

The album was full of photos of Granny doing ballet. Every single one made shivers go up my arms. I couldn't speak. I just wanted to keep staring and staring – Granny in a *plié* with the most perfect turnout in the world; Granny bending down to tie up her shoe with the straightest back in the world; Granny standing on *pointe* with the best arch I've ever seen. *My* granny. Doing ballet, just like I do, except about a million times better.

Then we came to the very last photo in the book. It took up nearly the whole page.

Granny was wearing a long white ballet dress, her hair really scraped back with a little silver headdress, and she had make-up on. It was a beautiful picture and I couldn't take my eyes off it.

"I gave up shortly after that," she said in a quiet voice.

"But why? You must have been brilliant at it. Why did you give up?"

"I wasn't brilliant, love. *Good*, I'll grant you. But not brilliant. And there were girls out there who were better than I was. It was as simple as that. I knew in my heart that I'd never be good enough to be a ballerina. So I gave up."

"Oh, Granny. That's terrible. I bet you *could* have been a ballerina."

She didn't say anything, but I could still see tears in her eyes and I think they were new ones.

"*I* love ballet too," I told her, to try and cheer her up. "I'm really glad you gave me that present."

"I thought you would. That's why I wanted you to try it."

"But how could you tell I'd like it? Was it because I was good at gym?"

"No, it was just because you reminded me of *me* so much. I used to go careering around at top speed, just like you, always chasing after things and never stopping to smell the roses..."

"Smell the roses?"

"It's an expression. It means never appreciating the things around you. I thought ballet was stupid when I was about eight. I even teased some of the girls at school who did it. But then one day we went to a pantomime – *Jack and the Beanstalk* it was – and there was a scene with some ballet dancing. The dancers were supposed to be the sylphs of the clouds, and my brothers were huffing and puffing and scowling and muttering because they wanted to get on with the bit where the giant appeared. And I started imitating them like I always did. But then I realized that I was enjoying watching the dancing. And gradually as it went on, I got more and more excited about it. And the very second the curtain went down for the interval I started begging to be allowed to go to ballet classes. It took me nearly a year of pestering to get them."

"Wow!" I breathed. Then I didn't feel like saying anything at all for a while. I just wanted to think about all that Granny had told me, and try to imagine what it must have been like. So we went through the album again, only backwards this time, and when we were on the very first page I decided to tell Granny what had happened at the last ballet lesson.

"Miss Coralie says that all the extra gym I'm doing is having a bad effect on my ballet and I've got to make a decision about whether I'm going to concentrate on ballet or gym. But how can I choose when I love them both? You see, I keep thinking I'm in gym club when I'm really in ballet and then I think I'm in ballet when I'm at gym. And it makes me go all wrong. So I do stiff, straight arms for ballet and forget to turn out, and then I do soft arms for gym and run too gently and things like that, and both teachers get cross with me, but how am I supposed to remember what I'm doing? It's impossible to always get it right and..."

I could feel a lump in my throat but I never ever cry so I tried to swallow it down. But Granny put her arm round me and said, "Ssh, it's all right, love," into my hair and then I couldn't stop the tears coming out of my eyes, and next minute I was really crying and crying.

I tried to tell her that I'm not normally such a baby, but she just kept shushing me and saying that crying's good for you, and even boys sometimes do it in private. So in the end I gave in, and did great big sobs, but it didn't matter.

Then, just when I was blowing my nose, the phone rang and it was Mum wanting me to go back home, but Granny asked Mum if I could stay the night and I could tell what Mum was saying on the other end because of Granny's answers.

"No, she can use her finger to clean her teeth just this once... No, don't worry about bringing anything round, I'm sure I can find her something to wear in bed... All right, dear. I'll walk her round at eight-thirty when she's had her breakfast... Yes, dear... Yes, I'll make sure she's in bed nice and early... She's just sitting quietly with me and we're having a nice chat... Yes... All right, dear, bye bye."

I was so happy about staying the night. Now I'd got loads of time to talk to Granny. I smiled at her through my tears, then she went to get me some kitchen roll to wipe my face.

"That's better, isn't it?"

I nodded and did one of those sobby sighs that goes upwards.

"Right. First things first." She sat down on the

settee and told me to put my foot back on her lap. "This is the place, right?"

I nodded.

"We need to massage it gently in tiny circles and I think that will do the trick. I reckon this is the same injury that I had when I was fifteen and about to do a ballet exam. It was a physiotherapist who taught me how to massage across the tendons like this." Granny told me to watch carefully so that I could do it myself the next day. "With any luck, it'll be gone in a day or two if we do it thoroughly tonight and then again in the morning. And see if you can find a few minutes during the day to give it another little massage. It's not a bad sprain, otherwise you wouldn't be able to walk at all."

"But will I be able to do gym tomorrow?"

"Best not. You don't want to ruin your foot for the competition."

"Do you think it'll be better in time for the competition though?"

"I'll cross my fingers."

I gulped and went into a daydream, wondering what to say to Miss Banner. But Granny's voice brought me back. "Do you think Miss Coralie's right?"

"What, about having to choose between ballet and gym?"

She nodded.

"Yes…because the older I get the more extra gym I'll have to do. There are so many competitions, you see."

"And I presume you don't want to give it up."

"Well, everyone says I'm really good at it."

"That isn't what I asked. Why do you think Miss Coralie wants you to make a decision? Why doesn't she just let you carry on with ballet for fun and not worry too much if you forget where you are every so often? What's wrong with that?"

"Because she's fed up about the gym making me go wrong."

"But why should she mind so much?"

I didn't get what Granny was going on about. I shook my head slowly. "I don't know why."

"It's because she can see how good you are at ballet, and she's sad and cross because it looks as though you're going to specialize in gym. I expect Miss Coralie was hoping you might specialize in ballet. There was no need for her to say anything at all, was there? But she wanted to know how you were feeling."

I couldn't believe what Granny was saying. "Do you really think Miss Coralie thinks I'm good?"

"Yes. And she's right. You *are* good. I saw you in the show, and since then I've seen you practising and improving. I've patted myself on the back lots of times for getting you those lessons."

I just stared at the table and did some more thinking. It still brought me back to the same problem. "The trouble is, I've got too much gym all the time, and it's probably going to get more and more... But I don't want to give it up, and I *definitely* don't want to give up ballet."

"How does gym make you feel?"

"Really good. Like being on a fast ride at a theme park. At least...it used to..."

"*Used* to?"

I nodded.

Granny patted my leg. "Go and see how that foot feels now."

I went over to her windowsill taking careful steps, but on the third step I realized that I didn't have to worry. It was much better. Carefully I tried a *plié* and then a *rond de jambe* and then I came away from the windowsill and slowly raised my left leg in a low *arabesque*.

"How does it feel?"

"Miles better!"

"Good. Now, forget about your foot and tell me how the dancing made you feel?"

"I can't explain."

"Why not?"

"Because it's not like anything else. It's just...the best feeling in the whole world."

Granny looked at me with searching eyes and it was a moment before she spoke. "I never *did* tell you what happened to my long, straight, smooth-flowing river, did I?"

"No, and I've been dying to find out. Has it got something to do with ballet and gym, by any chance?"

"Well..."

9 The Competition

My foot was much better the next day. It still hurt a bit if I tried out a *changement* or anything jumpy, but whenever the teacher wasn't watching I did a bit of the massaging thing that Granny had taught me. All the same, I didn't dare do gym club and I knew Miss Banner was not going to be pleased.

"I don't know how I did it, Miss Banner... It just started hurting, and I don't want to strain it..."

"Hmm, well *I* can guess how you did it. I've warned you often enough about ballet, Rose." She shook her head and huffed and puffed as she looked at my feet and did the same massage that Granny had taught me. "Keep doing this at home and *no* ballet! Come and see me tomorrow, all right?"

I nodded. She could say what she liked about ballet, because Granny had sorted out the muddle in my head, so I just smiled and said nothing.

By the following Monday, my foot was completely better. On the Tuesday morning I told Mum I didn't want to go to ballet because I wanted to save all my energy and concentration for the gym competition.

"Sensible girl!" said Mum.

"Wonders will never cease!" said Dad.

"What time does the competition start on Saturday?" asked Rory.

"Two o'clock," said Mum.

"Do *I* have to go?" asked Adam for the tenth time.

"We'll see," said Mum.

✳

In the end, Adam did go. And at ten past three on Saturday afternoon, I was with Miss Banner and Sasha and Katie and all the other competitors from the other schools at one end of the massive sports hall. Mum and Dad and Granny were with Adam, Rory and Jack and the rest of the audience at the other end.

I was dying for the competition to start now and I think the audience was too. Everyone had stopped talking, silently waiting for the first vault. I wasn't at all nervous. In fact, I think Poppy and Jasmine were more nervous than me. They'd come running over when we were right in the middle of the warm-up and done a quick thumb-thumb, because Jasmine said that Poppy had been worrying that the last one we'd done hadn't been a proper one, as our thumbs hadn't been totally touching, and she didn't want to be the one to bring me bad luck.

We had to do two vaults each. Miss Banner

had decided that Sasha would go first. I was going to go last and my two vaults were a straddle and a handspring. Handsprings are the hardest, so they're marked out of ten. All the other types of vault are marked out of eight. But not many people risk handsprings because they're easier to mess up, so you might only get six or seven marks out of ten. Most gym teachers think it's best to stick to the easier vaults and try to get eight out of eight.

Our school was the last school to do the vaults and I was the very last person of all. Out of all the competitors only one other girl had done a handspring, but she'd slightly messed up the landing and only scored a six. The best school so far was Little Trent. All three girls had scored perfect eights for both their vaults. So they'd scored forty-eight points, which was absolutely brilliant.

The moment I realized that, I started to get nervous. It was strange because I'm never usually nervous about anything. It made my shoulders go stiff and I had to keep rolling them round and round to get them loose again.

My nervousness disappeared when I was in my start position. I just wanted to get on with it. I ran hard and gave it loads of attack on the vault, and the landing felt fine. As I did my presentation at the end the audience clapped and I wondered if their hands were beginning to hurt because they'd had to do so much clapping. I was so busy thinking about that as I walked back up to the start that I forgot to look at the judges' mark, so I had to ask Miss Banner what it was when I got back.

"You scored eight, Rose! Well done!"

A moment later, Sasha was pounding towards the vault for the second time. I heard Miss Banner whisper "Yes!" to herself as Sasha went into her straddle, and then a bigger "Yess!" when the audience clapped her landing.

Sasha and Katie both scored eights and then

it was my turn again. I did my starting presentation and imagined I was giving myself an injection of *oomph*, then set off really fast. The feeling I had, as I did my flight off, was as good as being on a big dipper. I flung my arms back hard and didn't wobble at all as the clapping started.

"Yessss!" came a loud voice from the audience and I realized it was Adam. He was clapping over his head and so was Rory. Jack was stabbing the air to make me look at the judges. I couldn't believe my eyes. They were holding up a nine. We were level with Little Trent now. I looked back at the audience and saw Mum half-laughing and half-crying and Dad gave me a massive thumbs up. Poppy and Jasmine were so busy thumb-thumbing each other that they didn't even see me looking. And Granny had a big beam on her face. She gave me a little wave and I gave her one back.

After that it was the floor work. The schools

had to go in the same order and we were all using the same music. I thought the first school did a really good routine because they made it lovely and floaty, but the judges only gave them a six.

Miss Banner spoke to me in an urgent hiss. "You know why that school was marked down, don't you?"

"Because it was too much like ballet?"

"Exactly!"

"Well, if I'd been a judge I would have given them ten," I told her.

Katie and Sasha giggled but Miss Banner didn't look very pleased. "Make sure you don't start softening the movements when it's our turn, Rose, that's all!"

I wasn't going to soften them. I didn't want to. This was gym, not ballet. I was going to be straight and strong with parallel lines and no turnout.

The second and third schools both scored

eight and Little Trent scored nine. It was no wonder because they had really difficult skills in their routine and I didn't see a single thing go wrong.

"I would have given *them* ten, too," I told Miss Banner.

"It's a good job you're not the judge then, because that would make them impossible to beat!"

"Oh, yes. I hadn't thought of that!" And I hadn't.

The fifth school scored seven and then it was our turn. Just before the music started, when Sasha, Katie and I were in our positions, you could hear loads of sounds that you'd never normally notice. They came out loudly against the silence. I knew I shouldn't be thinking about things like that because it stopped me from focusing. So I pretended to be injecting myself with *oomph* again and then the music started. Katie didn't seem at all nervous any more.

She'd already told me that she likes it better when it's all three of us because then she doesn't feel as though it's her fault if it goes wrong.

But we didn't go wrong. In fact, I think we did it better than we'd ever done it before and when I landed in the splits and the other two were in their finishing shapes, the audience cheered and whistled as well as clapping. Well, there was *one* whistle and I think it was Dad actually.

We didn't have to wait at all for the judges to give their mark. They just looked at each other, nodded and held up a ten. I heard another gasp, only this time it came from me! We'd won! We'd actually won! It was unbelievable!

And now it was all over we were allowed to do what we wanted. We didn't have to behave properly because it didn't matter any more. Sasha and Katie were jumping up and down hugging each other and trying to get me to join in the hug. I joined in for a few seconds, then I went towards the audience and Poppy and

Jasmine came rushing down so we three could do our own hug.

"You were the best, Rose!" said Jasmine. "I mean, I already knew you were brilliant, but I've never seen you do a proper display and I couldn't believe all those things you can do."

And then Miss Banner came over. "Well done, Rose. You were so strong and so spot on all the way through." She looked up into the audience. "Here comes your family. My goodness, you've got a lot of fans, haven't you!"

"This is my granny," I told Miss Banner, holding Granny's hand and pulling her forwards because she was stuck behind Jack.

"Pleased to meet you," said Miss Banner.

I looked round and saw that the whole of the floor area was full of gymnasts and audience all mixed up. The talking was loud and excited because the final marks had been put up on the wall and everyone could see that our school had won.

"A bit of a star, you are, Rose!" said Dad, winking at Miss Banner.

"She certainly is," said Miss Banner. "That hard work paid off, didn't it, Rose?" She put her arm round me. "And the next competition should be even better, with all the extra classes."

Mum hugged me. "Well done, love!"

"We'll have you in those Olympic Games yet!" laughed Dad.

"I bet you *could*, you know Ro!" said Adam, and Jack and Rory both started agreeing with him.

I looked at Granny. Her eyes were twinkling, just like they had done when she'd told me about the long, straight river. I suddenly knew that now was the time for me to say something.

"I don't want to be in the Olympic Games, Adam."

Everyone looked at me. Miss Banner laughed. "Well, not just yet, anyway!"

That made everyone laugh.

"No, not ever."

"How about the European Games then?" said Dad.

This time, no one laughed. I think they must have seen the serious look on my face. I caught sight of Jasmine's huge eyes. I'd told her and Poppy how I felt and what I was going to say when the time came and they'd both hugged me and said I was so brave. I didn't feel brave. I just felt right because nothing was mixed up in my head any more. I could still hear Granny's voice inside my head telling me about the long, straight, smooth-flowing river that was her life, and how it all changed when she was seventeen.

"I suddenly knew in my heart that I wasn't good enough to be a ballerina and if I couldn't be a ballerina, I didn't want to have anything more to do with ballet. Everyone said I'd regret it, and tried to persuade me to be a teacher, and talked about what a waste of time my ballet lessons had been. But I knew they hadn't.

They'd been the river of my life – the long, straight, smooth-flowing river, but the river was branching into two and the ballet bit was turning into a stream that would become more a gentle backwater. Somewhere beautiful, that would always be a haven, but no longer part of the main stream of my life. Your grandad came along shortly after that. He was the biggest stream of all and he stayed with me for longer than any other stream.

Your river, pet, was a long, straight gym river, until the ballet stream came along to join it. But you don't need anyone to tell you which is more important to you. All you have to do is close your eyes and feel the pull of the current and then you'll know. Just like I did."

I turned to Miss Banner. "I don't want to do any more competitions, Miss Banner. I really like gym and I don't want to give it up, but I don't like it as much as I like ballet, so I only want to do gym club from now on."

All over the hall the hubbub of people talking and laughing went on, but in our little circle there was a horrible silence. No one liked what I'd said. I began to feel the teensiest bit nervous and I looked at Granny to check that I hadn't been cheeky or anything. Her eyes were still twinkling and it made my nervousness go away. Then Poppy and Jasmine came and stood on either side of me. The triplegang together.

Adam was first to speak. "You're mad!"

"Stark raving bonkers," added Rory.

"Well, I think it's cool," said Jack. "Let her do what she wants, poor kid."

"No one's going to make you do extra gym if you don't want to, love," said Mum. But there was a sad look in her eyes.

Dad was frowning. "You'd be a fool to waste that talent, Rose."

"Well, we can cross that bridge when we come to it," said Miss Banner, smiling brightly. "I must pop over and say hello to Sasha's and

Katie's families now."

I don't think she believed that I meant what I'd just said. Or maybe she thought I'd change my mind by the time it came to the next competition. But I wouldn't. I was certain of that. In fact, I'd never been so certain of anything in my whole life.

Granny winked at me and I remembered what she'd said when she'd come up to say night night to me.

"You see, you ARE like that Russian doll, pet. You had so much inside you, and now you're starting to find it all!"

10 The Best Feeling in the World

"And *one* and *two* and *three* and *four*..."

I was wearing my lovely new leotard that Granny had bought me, and I felt like a bird that had been trapped in a cage and was now flying around the sky. No way could the big dipper ever feel this good. We were doing the *port de bras* and it was lovely to be using soft arms. Poppy and Jasmine had helped me a lot with this exercise and I knew I was doing it better than I'd ever done it before.

At the beginning of the lesson Miss Coralie

had asked me if I was quite better now after missing class last week, and I'd told her that I hadn't been ill, I'd just had too much gym to do for the competition. She'd asked me how I'd got on in the competition and I'd told her that our school had won.

"Wonderful! Well done!" she'd said, but I'd seen that same sad look in her eyes that I'd seen in Mum's.

"*Tendu* to second and close in fifth..." Miss Coralie had been walking along the rows but she stopped in front of me and watched me till we'd finished on the first side, then said, "Nice, Rose", and carried on watching me while we all did it on the other side.

"You've been working hard," she said, when the music finished. Her eyes were very bright.

"It's because the competition's over so now I'm back to ballet."

"Until the next competition?" she said quietly.

"I'm not doing any more competitions. I thought about what you said and I've made my decision. I want to concentrate on ballet."

She smiled a proper smile and quite a few girls stared at me. Then we carried on to the next exercise just as if nothing had happened. Miss Coralie stood at the front and watched the class in general. I loved doing the *arabesque*. I'd worked hard at getting my placing exactly right and I could feel Miss Coralie's eyes on me again. Everything just flowed and flowed until I held my final position and heard the best words in the world.

"Lovely, Rose!"

The feeling was so big, I thought it might burst out of me, but I was determined to hold it tight inside until I passed Jazz and Poppy in the line.

I couldn't wait to see the looks on their faces when I told them.

Basic Ballet Positions

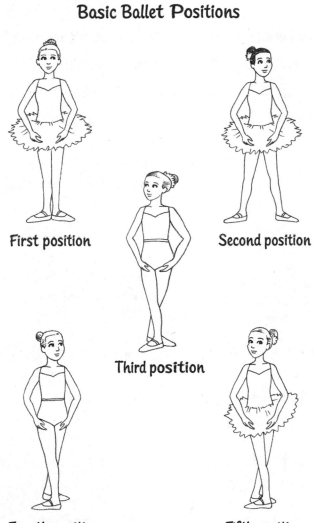

First position

Second position

Third position

Fourth position

Fifth position

Ballet words are mostly in French, which makes them more magical. But when you're learning, it's nice to know what they mean too. Here are some of the words that all Miss Coralie's students have to learn:

adage The name for the slow steps in the centre of the room, away from the *barre*.

arabesque A beautiful balance on one leg.

assemblé A jump where the feet come together at the end.

battement dégagé A foot exercise at the *barre* to get beautiful toes.

battement tendu Another foot exercise where you stretch your foot until it points.

chassé A soft smooth slide of the feet.

echappé This one's impossible to describe, but it's like your feet escaping from each other!

fifth position croisé When you are facing, say the *left* corner, with your feet in fifth position, and your front foot is the *right* foot.

fouetté This step is so fast your feet are in a blur! You do it to prepare for *pirouettes*.

grand battement High kick!

jeté A spring where you land on the opposite foot. Rose loves these!

pas de bourrée Tiny little steps to the side, like a mouse.

pas de chat A cat hop from one foot to the other.

plié This is the first step we do in class. You have to bend your knees slowly and make sure your feet are turned right out, with your heels firmly planted on the floor for as long as possible.

port de bras Arm movements, which Poppy is good at.

révérence The curtsey at the end of class.

rond de jambe This is where you make a circle with your leg.

sissonne A scissor step.

sissonne en arrière A scissor step going backwards. This is really hard!

sissonne en avant A scissor step going forwards.

soubresaut A jump off two feet, pointing your feet hard in the air.

temps levé A step and sweep up the other leg then jump.

turnout You have to stand with your legs and feet and hips all opened out and pointing to the side, not the front. This is the most important thing in ballet that everyone learns right from the start.